Address Unknown

Address Unknown

—

Kressmann Taylor

ISBN: 1518869769
ISBN 13: 9781518869761

2016 Foreword To
Address Unknown

—————

WHEN "ADDRESS UNKNOWN" WAS FIRST published in the United States, in *STORY* magazine in September 1938, it caused an immediate sensation. Written as a series of letters between a Jewish American living in San Francisco and his former business partner, returned to Germany, the story, early on, exposed the poison of Nazism to the American public.

Within ten days of publication, the entire printing of that issue of *STORY* was sold out, and enthusiastic readers were mimeographing copies of the story to send to friends. National radio commentator Walter Winchell heartily recommended the story as "the best piece of the month, something you shouldn't miss," and *Readers Digest* put aside its long-standing no-fiction rule to reprint the piece for its more than three million readers.

In 1939, Simon & Schuster published *ADDRESS UNKNOWN* as a book and sold fifty thousand copies, a huge number in those years. Hamish Hamilton followed suit in England with a British edition, and foreign translations were begun. But 1939 was also the year of *Blitzkrieg*; within months most of Europe was under the domination of Adolph Hitler, the Dutch translation disappeared, and the only other European appearance of *ADDRESS UNKNOWN* was on the Reichskommisars list of banned books. So the story remained unknown on the continent for the next sixty years, despite its great impact and success in the U.S. and England.

Author Kressmann Taylor, "the woman who jolted America," was born Kathrine Kressmann in Portland, Oregon in 1903. After graduating from the University of Oregon in 1924, she moved to San Francisco and worked as an advertising copywriter, in her spare time writing for some small literary journals. In 1928 the editors of the *San Francisco Review*, a magazine she particularly liked, invited her to a party where she met Elliott Taylor, the owner of his own advertising agency, and they were married within two weeks. In 1932, when the Great Depression had put an end to the advertising industry, the couple bought a small farm in southern Oregon, where they literally lived off the land, growing their own food and panning gold, taking their two small children and adding a third in 1935.

In 1938 they moved to New York, where Elliott worked as an editor, and Kathrine finished writing *Address Unknown*. Elliott showed it to *STORY* magazine editor Whit Burnett, who immediately wished to publish it. He and Elliott decided that the story was too strong to appear under the name of a woman, and assigned Kathrine the literary pseudonym Kressmann Taylor, a professional name she accepted and kept for the rest of her life, largely because of the success of *Address Unknown*. This is how she describes the original motivation for the story:

> *A short time before the war, some cultivated, intellectual, warm-hearted German friends of mine returned to Germany after living in the United States. In a very short time they turned into sworn Nazis. They refused to listen to the slightest criticism about Hitler. During a return visit to California, they met an old dear friend of theirs on the street, who had been very close to them and who was a Jew. They did not speak to him. They turned their backs on him when he held his hands out to embrace them. How can such a thing happen, I wondered. What changed their hearts so? What steps brought them to such cruelty?*

These questions haunted me very much and I could not forget them. It was hard to believe that these people whom I knew and respected had fallen victim to the Nazi poison. I began researching Hitler and reading his speeches and the writings of his advisors. What I discovered was terrifying. What worried me most was that no one in America was aware of what was happening in Germany, and they also did not care. In 1938, the isolationist movement in America was strong; the politicians said that affairs in Europe were none of our business and that Germany was fine. Even Charles Lindbergh came back from Germany saying how wonderful the people were. But there were some students who returned from studying in Germany and they told the truth about the Nazi atrocities. When their fraternity brothers had thought it would be fun to send them letters making fun of Hitler, they had written back and said, "Stop it. We're in danger. These people don't fool around. You could murder one of these Nazis by writing letters to him."

When that incident occurred, it made only a small article in the news, but it caught Elliott's eye; he brought it home to Kathrine, and it gave rise to their joint idea of using a letter as a weapon. She took that idea and went to work on the story she wanted to write.

I wanted to write about what the Nazis were doing and show the American public what happens to real, living people swept up in a warped ideology.

The result was *ADDRESS UNKNOWN*, a great success about which the *New York Times Book Review* stated in 1939, "This modern story is perfection itself. It is the most effective indictment of Nazism to appear in fiction." That indictment continued in her next book, *Until That Day*, published in 1942, (and reissued as *Day of No Return* in 2003)

Following the war, when any further indictment of the Nazis seemed no longer necessary, *Address Unknown* slipped from public notice and was largely forgotten, other then its inclusion in an occasional anthology.

Elliott Taylor died in 1953, and Kathrine lived as a widow for the next 15 years, continuing to write and to teach writing, journalism, and humanities at Gettysburg College, in Pennsylvania. Retiring in 1966, she moved to Florence, Italy, where she experienced the great flood of the Arno River in November of that year, which inspired her third book, *Diary of Florence in Flood* (aka *Ordeal by Water* in UK), published to critical acclaim in both England and America the following spring.

En route to Italy in 1966 on the Italian Lines *Michelangelo*, Kathrine met the American sculptor John Rood. The two felt an immediate attraction, had a shipboard romance, and were married the following year in Minneapolis, where he made his home. Thereafter, they lived part of each year in Minneapolis, part in the Val de Pesa, outside Florence. Even after Rood's death in 1974, Kathrine kept both homes for nearly twenty years, living quietly in each six months a year, simply as Mrs. John Rood.

Then, in 1995, when she was 91 years old, Story Press reissued *Address Unknown*, to commemorate the 50th anniversary of the liberation of the concentration camps, and because, as *STORY* editor Lois Rosenthal wrote, "its significant and timeless message has earned it a permanent place on the bookshelves of America." The book was well-received, and Kathrine, happily signing copies and granting television and press interviews, was gratified at its re-emergence, this time with the stature of a classic of American literature.

Kathrine Kressmann Taylor Rood died the following year, in July 1996, late in her 93rd year, sharp-witted, perceptive, and enthusiastic, even about the end of life. "Dying," she said in her last week, "is normal. It's as normal as being born." And she was ready. She had lived several successful lives: as a wife and mother, as a popular professor, and as the author of four books and a dozen short stories, one of which, *Address Unknown*, had been recognized as a classic while she lived.

Shortly after her death, a copy of the 1995 reissue came into the hands of French publisher Henri Dougier, of Editions Autrement, Paris. He saw at once its relevance to the entire European community, both those who had lived under the Nazi domination and those who needed to know what it had been like. He determined that a French translation must be undertaken, and that translation, by Michele Levy-Bram, hit the French bestseller list in late 1999. *Inconnu a cette adresse* sold 50,000 copies that first year; 100,000 the next, and another 450,000 since, selling far more than it ever had in the United States. Soon other Europeans were reading it, calling for its translation and publication in their own languages: Spanish, Catalan, Gallego, Basque, Italian, Dutch, German, Norwegian, Swedish, Danish, Portuguese, Polish, Czech, and then to the rest of the world as well: in Greek, Turkish, Korean, Chinese, Japanese, and others, (23 languages to date).

The great success of *Address Unknown* in book form has led to other successes: audio books in German, Italian, and French; radio productions in England, France, Israel, and Croatia; live theater productions in France, Israel, Turkey, Italy, Belgium, Holland, Argentina, the US, including off-Broadway in 2004, and in both French and English at the Soho Theatre in London in 2013.

It is exciting to see this little book recognized as a classic, and it is gratifying that Kathrine lived to see its recognition as such with the 1995 F&W edition, and to authorize in her last year the first of many translations -- into Hebrew, by the noted scholar/translator Asher Tarmon of Israel.

What the world will know of this story in future generations is hard to imagine, but it now seems that it will survive and will be included in the significant literature of the 20th century.

Prof. Charles Douglas Taylor
son of Kressmann Taylor

Contents

Address Unknown

———

SCHULSE-EISENSTEIN GALLERIES
SAN FRANCISCO, CALIFORNIA, U.S.A.

November 12, 1932

Herrn Martin Schulse
Schloss Rantzenburg
Munich, Germany

My Dear Martin:

Back in Germany! How I envy you! Although I have not seen it since my school days, the spell of *Unter den Linden* is still strong upon me -- the breadth of intellectual freedom, the discussions, the music, the light-hearted comradeship. And now the old Junker spirit, the Prussian arrogance and militarism are gone. You go to a democratic Germany, a land with a deep culture and the beginnings of a fine political freedom. It will be a good life. Your new address is impressive and I rejoice that the crossing was so pleasant for Elsa and the young sprouts.

As for me, I am not so happy. Sunday morning finds me a lonely bachelor without aim. My Sunday home is now transported over the wide seas. The big old house on the hill -- your welcome that said the day was not complete until we were together again! And our

1

dear jolly Elsa, coming out beaming, grasping my hand and shouting "Max, Max!" and hurrying indoors to open my favorite *Schnapps*. The fine boys, too, especially your handsome young Heinrich; he will be a grown man before I set eyes upon him again.

And dinner -- shall I evermore hope to eat as I have eaten? Now I go to a restaurant and over my lonely roast beef come visions of *gebackner Schinken* steaming in its Burgundy sauce, of *Spatzle,* ah! of *Spatzle* and *Spargel!* No, I shall never again become reconciled to my American diet. And the wines, so carefully slipped ashore from the German boats, and the pledges we made as the glasses brimmed for the fourth and fifth and sixth times.

Of course you are right to go. You have never become American despite your success here, and now that the business is so well established you must take your sturdy German boys back to the homeland to be educated. Elsa too has missed her family through the long years and they will be glad to see you as well. The impecunious young artist has now become the family benefactor, and that too will give you a quiet little triumph.

The business continues to go well. Mrs. Levine has bought the small Picasso at our price, for which I congratulate myself, and I have old Mrs. Fleshman playing with the notion of the hideous Madonna. No one ever bothers to tell her that any particular piece of hers is bad, because they are all so bad. However I lack your fine touch in selling to the old Jewish matrons. I can persuade them of the excellence of the investment, but you alone had the fine spiritual approach to a piece of art that unarmed them. Besides they probably never entirely trust another Jew.

A delightful letter came yesterday from Griselle. She writes that she is about to make me proud of my little sister. She has the lead in a new play in Vienna and the notices are excellent -- her discouraging years with the small companies are beginning to bear fruit. Poor child, it has not been easy for her, but she has never complained. She has a fine spirit, as well as beauty, and I hope the talent as well. She asked about you, Martin, in a very friendly way. There is no bitterness left there, for that passes quickly when one is young as she is. A few years and there is only a memory of the hurt, and of course neither of you was to be blamed. Those things are like quick storms, for a moment you are drenched and blasted, and you are so wholly helpless before them. But then the sun comes, and although you have neither quite forgotten, there remains only gentleness and no sorrow. You would not have had it otherwise, nor would I. I have not written Griselle that you are in Europe but perhaps I shall if you think it wise, for she does not make friends easily and I know she would be glad to feel that friends are not far away.

Fourteen years since the war! Did you mark the date? What a long way we have traveled, as peoples, from that bitterness! Again, my dear Martin, let me embrace you in spirit, and with the most affectionate remembrances to Elsa and the boys, believe me,

Your ever most faithful,
Max

S C H L O S S R A N T Z E N B U R G
M U N I C H, G E R M A N Y

December 10, 1932

Mr. Max Eisenstein
Schulse-Eisenstein Galleries
San Francisco, California, U.S.A.

Max, Dear Old Fellow:

The check and accounts came through promptly, for which my thanks. You need not send me such details of the business. You know how I am in accord with your methods, and here at Munich I am in a rush of new activities. We are established, but what a turmoil! The house, as you know, I had long in mind. And I got it at an amazing bargain. Thirty rooms and about ten acres of park; you would never believe it. But then, you could not appreciate how poor is now this sad land of mine. The servants' quarters, stables and outbuildings are most extensive, and would you believe it, we employ now ten servants for the same wages of our two in the San Francisco home.

The tapestries and pieces we shipped make a rich show and some other fine furnishings I have been able to secure, so that we are much admired, I was almost to say envied. Four full services in the finest china I have bought and much crystal, as well as a full service of silver for which Elsa is in ecstasies.

And for Elsa -- such a joke! You will, I know, laugh with me. I have purchased for her a huge bed. Such a size as never was before, twice the bigness of a double bed, and with great posters in carved wood. The sheets I must have made to order, for there are no sheets made that could fit it. And they are of linen, the finest linen sheets. Elsa laughs and laughs, and her old *Grossmutter* stands shaking her head and grumbles, "*Nein,* Martin, *nein.* You have made it so and now you must take care or she will grow to match it."

"*Ja*," says Elsa, "five more boys and I will fit it just nice and snug." And she will, Max.

For the boys there are three ponies (little Karl and Wolfgang are not big enough to ride yet) and a tutor. Their German is very bad, being too much mixed with English.

Elsa's family do not find things so easy now. The brothers are in the professions and, while much respected, must live together in one house. To the family we seem American millionaires, and while we are far from that yet our American income places us among the wealthy here. The better foods are high in price and there is much political unrest even now under the presidency of Hindenburg, a fine liberal whom I much admire.

Already old acquaintances urge me that I interest myself in administrative matters in the town. This I take under consideration. It may be somewhat to our benefit locally if I become an official.

As for you, my good Max, we have left you alone, but you must not become a misanthrope. Get yourself at once a nice fat little wife who will busy herself with all your cares and feed you into a good humor. That is my advice and it is good, although I smile as I write it.

You write of Griselle. So she wins her success, the lovely one! I rejoice with you, although even now I resent it that she must struggle to win her way, a girl alone. She was made, as any man can see, for luxury and for devotion and the charming and beautiful life where ease allows much play of the sensibilities. A gentle, brave soul is in her dark eyes, but there is something strong as iron and very daring too. She is a woman who does nothing and gives nothing lightly. Alas, dear Max, as always, I betray myself. But although you were silent during our stormy affair, you know that the decision was not easy for me. You never reproached me, your friend, while the little sister suffered, and I have always felt you knew that I suffered too, most gravely. What could I do? There was Elsa and my little sons. No other decision was possible to make. Yet for Griselle I keep a tenderness that will last long after she has taken a much younger man for husband or lover. The old wound has healed but the scar throbs at times, my friend.

I wish that you will give her our address. We are such a short distance from Vienna that she can feel there is for her a home close at hand. Elsa, too, knows nothing of the old feeling between us and you know with what warmth she would welcome your sister, as she would welcome you. Yes, you must tell her that we are here and urge her to soon make a contact with us. Give her our most warm congratulations for the fine success that she is making.

Elsa asks that I send to you her love, and Heinrich would also say "hello" to Uncle Max. We do not forget you, Maxel.

My heartiest greetings to you,
Martin

SCHULSE-EISENSTEIN GALLERIES
SAN FRANCISCO, CALIFORNIA, U.S.A.

January 21, 1933

Herrn Martin Schulse
Schloss Rantzenburg
Munich, Germany

My Dear Martin:

I was glad to forward your address to Griselle. She should have it shortly, if she has not already received it. What jollification there will be when she sees you all! I shall be with you in spirit as heartily as if I also could rejoin you in person.

You speak of the poverty there. Conditions have been bad here this winter, but of course we have known nothing of the privations you see in Germany.

Personally, you and I are lucky that we have such a sound following for the gallery. Of course our own clientele are cutting their purchases but if they buy only half as much as before we shall be comfortable, not extravagantly so, but very comfortable. The oils you sent are excellent, and the prices are amazing. I shall dispose of them at an appalling profit almost at once. And the ugly Madonna is gone! Yes, to old Mrs. Fleshman. How I gasped at her perspicacity in recognizing its worth, hesitating to set a price! She suspected me of having another client, and I named an indecent figure. She pounced on it, grinning slyly as she wrote her check. How I exulted as she bore the horror off with her, you alone will know.

Alas, Martin, I often am ashamed of myself for the delight I take in such meaningless little triumphs. You in Germany, with your country house and your affluence displayed before Elsa's relatives, and I in America, gloating because I have tricked a giddy old woman into buying a monstrosity. What a fine climax for two men of forty! Is it

7

for this we spend our lives, to scheme for money and then to strut it publicly? I am always castigating myself, but I continue to do as before. Alas, we are all caught in the same mill. We are vain and we are dishonest because it is necessary to triumph over other vain and dishonest persons. If I do not sell Mrs. Fleshman our horror, somebody else will sell her a worse one. We must accept these necessities.

But there is another realm where we can always find something true, the fireside of a friend, where we shed our little conceits and find warmth and understanding, where small selfishnesses are impossible and where wine and books and talk give a different meaning to existence. There we have made something that no falseness can touch. We are at home.

Who is this Adolf Hitler who seems rising toward power in Germany? I do not like what I read of him.

Embrace all the young fry and our abundant Elsa for

Your ever affectionate,
Max

SCHLOSSRANTZENBURG
MUNICH, GERMANY

March 25, 1933

Mr. Max Eisenstein
Schulse-Eisenstein Galleries
San Francisco, California, U.S.A.

Dear Old Max:

You have heard of course of the new events in Germany, and you will want to know how it appears to us here on the inside. I tell you truly, Max, I think in many ways Hitler is good for Germany, but I am not sure. He is now the active head of the government. I doubt much that even Hindenburg could now remove him from power, as he was truly forced to place him there. The man is like an electric shock, strong as only a great orator and a zealot can be. But I ask myself, is he quite sane? His brown shirt troops are of the rabble. They pillage and have started a bad Jew-baiting. But these may be minor things, the little surface scum when a big movement boils up. For I tell you, my friend, there is a surge -- a surge. The people everywhere have had a quickening. You feel it in the streets and shops. The old despair has been thrown aside like a forgotten coat. No longer the people wrap themselves in shame; they hope again. Perhaps there may be found an end to this poverty. Something, I do not know what, will happen. A leader is found! Yet cautiously to myself I ask, a leader to where? Despair overthrown often turns us in mad directions.

Publicly, as is natural, I express no doubt. I am now an official and a worker in the new regime and I exult very loud indeed. All of us officials who cherish whole skins are quick to join the National Socialists. That is the name for Herr Hitler's party. But also it is not only expedient, there is something more, a feeling that we of Germany have found our destiny and that the future sweeps toward us in an overwhelming wave. We too must move. We must go with it. Even now there are being wrongs done. The storm troopers are having their moment of victory, and there are bloody heads and sad hearts to show for it. But these things pass; if the end in view is right they pass and are forgotten. History writes a clean new page.

All I now ask myself, and I can say to you what I cannot say to any here is: Is the end right? Do we make for a better goal? For you know, Max, I have seen these people of my race since I came here, and I have learned what agonies they have suffered, what years of less and less bread, of leaner bodies, of the end of hope. The quicksand of despair held them, it was at their chins. Then just before they died a man came and pulled them out. All they now know is, they will not die. They are in hysteria of deliverance, almost they worship him. But whoever the savior was, they would have done the same. God grant it is a true leader and no black angel they follow so joyously. To you alone, Max, I say I do not know. I do not know. Yet I hope.

So much for politics. Ourselves, we delight in our new home and have done much entertaining. Tonight the mayor is our guest, at a dinner for twenty-eight. We spread ourselves a little, maybe, but that is to be forgiven. Elsa has a new gown of blue velvet, and is in terror for fear it will not be big enough. She is with child again. There is the way to keep a wife contented, Max. Keep her so busy with babies she has no time to fret.

Our Heinrich has made a social conquest. He goes out on his pony and gets himself thrown off, and who picks him up but the Baron Von Freische. They have a long conversation about America, and one day the baron calls and we have coffee. Heinrich will go there to lunch next week. What a boy! It is too bad his German is not better but he delights everyone.

So we go, my friend, perhaps to become part of great events, perhaps only to pursue our simple family way, but never abandoning that trueness of friendship of which you speak so movingly. Our hearts go out to you across the wide sea, and when the glasses are filled we toast "Uncle Max."

Yours in affectionate regard,
Martin

SCHULSE-EISENSTEIN GALLERIES
SAN FRANCISCO, CALIFORNIA, U.S.A.

May 18, 1933

Herrn Martin Schulse
Schloss Rantzenburg
Munich, Germany

Dear Martin:

I am in distress at the press reports that come pouring in to us from the Fatherland. Thus it is natural that I turn to you for light while there are only conflicting stories to be had here. I am sure things cannot be as bad as they are pictured. A terrible pogrom, that is the consensus of our American papers.

I know your liberal mind and warm heart will tolerate no viciousness and that from you I can have the truth. Aaron Silberman's son has just returned from Berlin and had, I hear, a narrow escape. The tales he tells of what he has seen, floggings, the forcing of quarts of castor oil through clenched teeth and the consequent hours of dying through the slow agony of bursting guts, are not pretty ones. These things may be true, and they may, as you have said, be but the brutal surface froth of human revolution. Alas, to us Jews they are a sad story familiar through centuries of repetition, and it is almost unbelievable that the old martyrdom must be endured in a civilized nation today. Write me, my friend, and set my mind at ease.

Griselle's play will come to a close about the end of June after a great success. She writes that she has an offer for another role in Vienna and also for a very fine one in Berlin for the autumn. She is talking most of the latter one, but I have written her to wait until the anti-Jewish feeling has abated. Of course she uses another name which is not Jewish (Eisenstein would be impossible for the stage anyway), but it is not her name that would betray her origin. Her features, her gestures, her emotional voice proclaim her a Jewess no matter what she calls herself, and if this feeling has any real strength she had best not venture into Germany just at present.

Forgive me, my friend, for so distrait and brief a letter but I cannot rest until you have reassured me. You will, I know, write in all fairness. Pray do so at once.

With the warmest protestations of faith and friendship for you and yours, I am ever your faithful

Max

Deutsch-Bolkische Bank und Handelsgesellschaft,
Munchen

July 9, 1933

Mr. Max Eisenstein
Schulse-Eisenstein Galleries
San Francisco, California, U.S.A.

Dear Max:

You will see that I write upon the stationery of my bank. This is necessary because I have a request to make of you and I wish to avoid the new censorship which is most strict. We must for the present discontinue writing each other. It is impossible for me to be in correspondence with a Jew even if it were not that I have an official position to maintain. If a communication becomes necessary you must enclose it with the bank draft and not write to me at my house again.

As for the stern measures that so distress you, I myself did not like them at first, but I have come to see their painful necessity. The Jewish race is a sore spot to any nation that harbors it. I have never hated the individual Jew -- yourself I have always cherished as a friend, but you will know that I speak in all honesty when I say I have loved you, not because of your race but in spite of it.

The Jew is the universal scapegoat. This does not happen without reason, and it is not the old superstition about Christ-killers that makes them distrusted. But this Jew trouble is only an incident. Something bigger is happening.

If I could show you, if I could make you see -- the rebirth of this new Germany under our Gentle Leader! Not for always can the world grind a great people down in subjugation. In defeat for fourteen years we bowed our heads. We ate the bitter bread of shame and drank the thin gruel of poverty. But now we are free men. We rise in our might and hold our heads up before the nations. We purge our bloodstream of its baser elements. We go singing through our valleys with strong muscles tingling for a new work -- and from the mountains ring the voices of Wodan and Thor, the old, strong gods of the German race.

But no. I am sure as I write, as with the new vision my own enthusiasm burns, that you will not see how necessary is all this for Germany. You will see only that your own people are troubled. You will not see that a few must suffer for the millions to be saved. You will be a Jew first and wail for your people. This I understand. It is the Semitic character. You lament but you are never brave enough to fight back. That is why there are pogroms.

Alas, Max, this will pain you, I know, but you must realize the truth. There are movements far bigger than the men who make them up. As for me, I am a part of the movement. Heinrich is an officer in the boys' corps, which is headed by Baron Von Freische, whose rank is now shedding a luster upon our house, for he comes often to visit with Heinrich and Elsa, whom he much admires. Myself, I am up to the ears in work. Elsa concerns herself little with politics except to adore our Gentle Leader. She gets tired too easily this last month. Perhaps the babies come too fast. It will be better for her when this one is born.

I regret our correspondence must close this way, Max. Perhaps we can someday meet again on a field of better understanding.

As ever your,
Martin Schulse

SCHULSE-EISENSTEIN GALLERIES
SAN FRANCISCO, CALIFORNIA, U.S.A.

August 1, 1933

Herrn Martin Schulse
(kindness of J. Lederer)
Schloss Rantzenburg
Munich, Germany

Martin, My Old Friend:

I am sending this by the hand of Jimmy Lederer, who will shortly
pass through Munich on a European vacation. I cannot rest after the
letter you last sent me. It is so unlike you I can only attribute its con-
tents to your fear of the censorship. The man I have loved as a brother,
whose heart has ever been brimming with sympathy and friendship,
cannot possibly partake of even a passive partnership in the butchery
of innocent people. I trust and pray that it may be so, that you will
write me no exposition, which might be dangerous for you, -- only a
simple "yes." That will tell me that you play the part of expediency but
that your heart has not changed, and that I was not deluded in believ-
ing you to be always a man of fine and liberal spirit to whom wrongs
are wrongs in whosoever's name they may be committed.

This censorship, this persecution of all men of liberal thought, the
burning of libraries and corruption of the universities would arouse
your antagonism if there had been no finger laid on one of my race in
Germany. You are a liberal, Martin. You have always taken the long
view. I know that you cannot be swept away from sanity by a popular movement which has so much that is bad about it, no matter how
strong it may be.

I can see why the Germans acclaim Hitler. They react against the
very real wrongs which have been laid on them since the disaster of
the war. But you, Martin, have been almost an American since the

war. I know that it is not my friend who has written to me, that it will prove to have been only the voice of caution and expediency.

Eagerly I await the one word that will set my heart at peace. Write your "yes" quickly.

My love to you all,
Max

Deutsch-Volkische Bank und Handelsgesellschaft,
München

August 18, 1933

Mr. Max Eisenstein
Schulse-Eisenstein Galleries
San Francisco, California, U.S.A.

Dear Max:

I have your letter. The word is "no." You are a sentimentalist. You do not know that all men are not cut to your pattern. You put nice little tags on them, like liberal and expect them to act so-and-so. But you are wrong. So, I am an American liberal? No! I am a German patriot.

A liberal is a man who does not believe in doing anything. He is a talker about the rights of man, but just a talker. He likes to make a big noise about freedom of speech, and what is freedom of speech? Just the chance to sit firmly on the backside and say that whatever is being done by the active men is wrong. What is so futile as the liberal? I know him well because I have been one. He condemns the passive government because it makes no change. But let a powerful man arise, let an active man start to make a change, then where is your liberal? He is against it. To the liberal any change is the wrong one.

He calls this the long view but it is merely a bad scare that he will have to do something himself. He loves words and high-sounding precepts but he is useless to the men who make the world what it is. These are the only important men, the doers. And here in Germany a doer has risen. A vital man is changing things. The whole tide of a people's life changes in a minute because the man of action has come. And I join him. I am not just swept along by a current. The useless life that was all talk and no accomplishment I drop. I put my back and shoulders behind the great new movement. I am a man because I act.

Before that I am just a voice. I do not question the ends of our action. It is not necessary. I know it is good because it is so vital. Men are not drawn into bad things with so much joy and eagerness.

You say we persecute men of liberal thought, we destroy libraries. You should wake from your musty sentimentalizing. Does the surgeon spare the cancer because he must cut to remove it? We are cruel. Of course we are cruel. As all birth is brutal, so is this new birth of ours. But we rejoice. Germany lifts high her head among the nations of the world. She follows her Glorious Leader to triumph. What can you know of this, you who only sit and dream? You have never known a Hitler. He is a drawn sword. He is a white light, but hot as the sun of a new day.

I must insist that you write no further. We are no longer in sympathy, as now we must both realize.

Martin Schulse

EISENSTEIN GALLERIES
SAN FRANCISCO, CALIFORNIA, U.S.A.

September 5, 1933

Herrn Martin Schulse
% Deutsch-Boelkische Bank
und Handelsgeselschaft
Munich, Germany

Dear Martin:

Enclosed are your draft and the month's accounts. It is of necessity that I send a brief message. Griselle has gone to Berlin. She is too daring. But she has waited so long for success she will not relinquish it, and laughs at my fears. She will be at the Koenig Theater. You are an official. For old friendship's sake, I beg of you to watch over her. Go to Berlin if you can and see whether she is in danger.

It will distress you to observe that I have been obliged to remove your name from the firm's name. You know who our principal clients are, and they will touch nothing now from a firm with a German name.

Your new attitude I cannot discuss. But you must understand me. I did not expect you would take up arms for my people because they are my people, but because you were a man who loved justice.

I commend my rash Griselle to you. The child does not realize what a risk she is taking. I shall not write again.

Goodbye, my friend,

Max

EISENSTEIN GALLERIES
SAN FRANCISCO, CALIFORNIA, U.S.A.

November 5, 1933

Herrn Martin Schulse
% Deutsch-Boelkische Bank
und Handelsgeselschaft
Munich, Germany

Martin:

I write again because I must. A black foreboding has taken possession of me. I wrote Griselle as soon as I knew she was in Berlin and she answered briefly. Rehearsals were going brilliantly; the play would open shortly. My second letter was more encouragement than warning, and it has been returned to me, the envelope unopened, marked only addressee unknown, (*Adressant Unbekannt*). What a darkness those words carry! How can she be unknown? It is surely a message that she has come to harm. They know what has happened to her, those stamped letters say, but I am not to know. She has gone into some sort of void and it will be useless to seek her. All this they tell me in two words, *Adressant Unbekannt*.

Martin, need I ask you to find her, to succor her? You have known her graciousness, her beauty and sweetness. You have had her love, which she has given to no other man. Do not attempt to write to me. I know I need not even ask you to aid. It is enough to tell you that something has gone wrong, that she must be in danger.

I leave her in your hands, for I am helpless.

Max

EISENSTEIN GALLERIES
SAN FRANCISCO, CALIFORNIA, U.S.A.

November 23, 1933

Herrn Martin Schulse
% Deutsch-Boelkische Bank
und Handelsgeselschaft
Munich, Germany

Martin:

I turn to you in despair. I could not wait for another month to pass so I am sending some information as to your investments. You may wish to make some changes and I can thus enclose my appeal with a bank letter.

It is Griselle. For two months there has been only silence from her, and now the rumors begin to come in to me. From Jewish mouth to Jewish mouth the tales slowly come back from Germany, tales so full of dread I would close my ears if I dared, but I cannot. I must be sure.

She appeared in the Berlin play for a week. Then she was jeered from the audience as a Jewess. She is so headstrong, so foolhardy, the splendid child! She threw the word back in their teeth. She told them proudly that she *was* a Jewess.

Some of the audience started after her. She ran backstage. Someone must have helped her for she got away with the whole pack at her heels and took refuge with a Jewish family in a cellar for several days. After that she changed her appearance as much as she could and started south, hoping to walk back to Vienna. She did not dare try the railroads. She told those she left that she would be safe if she could reach friends in Munich. That is my hope, that she has gone to you, for she has never reached Vienna. Send me word, Martin, and if she has not come there make a quiet investigation if you can. My mind cannot rest. I torture myself by day and by night, seeing the brave little thing trudging all those long miles through hostile country, with winter coming on. God grant you can send me a word of relief.

Max

Deutsch-Bolkische Bank und Handelsgesellschaft,
München

December 8, 1933

Heil Hitler! I much regret that I have bad news for you. Your sister is dead. Unfortunately she was, as you have said, very much a fool. Not quite a week ago she came here, with a bunch of storm troopers right behind her. The house was very active -- Elsa has not been well since little Adolf was born last month -- the doctor was here, and two nurses, with all the servants and children scurrying around.

By luck I answer the door. At first I think it is an old woman and then I see the face, and then I see the storm troopers have turned in the park gates. Can I hide her? It is one chance in thousands. A servant will be on us at any minute. Can I endure to have my house ransacked with Elsa ill in bed and to risk being arrested for harboring a Jew and to lose all I have built up here? Of course as a German I have one plain duty. She has displayed her Jewish body on the stage before pure young German men. I should hold her and turn her over to the storm troopers. But this I cannot do.

"You will destroy us all, Griselle," I tell her. "You must run back further in the park." She looks at me and smiles (she was always a brave girl) and makes her own choice.

"I would not bring you harm, Martin," she says, and she runs down the steps and out toward the trees. But she must be tired. She does not run very fast and the storm troopers have caught sight of her. I am helpless. I go in the house and in a few minutes she stops screaming, and in the morning I have the body sent down to the village for burial. She was a fool to come to Germany.

Poor little Griselle. I grieve with you, but as you see, I was helpless to aid her.

I must now demand you do not write again. Every word that comes to the house is now censored, and I cannot tell how soon they may start to open the mail to the bank. And I will no longer have any dealings with Jews, except for the receipt of money. It is not so good for me that a Jewess came here for refuge, and no further association can be tolerated.

A new Germany is being shaped here. We will soon show the world great things under our Glorious Leader.

Martin

CABLEGRAM

MUNICH JANUARY 2 1934

MARTIN SCHULSE

YOUR TERMS ACCEPTED NOVEMBER TWELVE AUDIT
SHOWS THIRTEEN PERCENT INCREASE FEBRUARY SECOND
FOURFOLD ASSURED PAN EXHIBITION MAY FIRST PREPARE
LEAVE FOR MOSCOW IF MARKET OPENS UNEXPECTEDLY
FINANCIAL INSTRUCTIONS MAILED NEW ADDRESS

EISENSTEIN

EISENSTEIN GALLERIES
SAN FRANCISCO, CALIFORNIA, U.S.A.

January 3, 1934

Herrn Martin Schulse
Schloss Rantzenburg
Munich, Germany

Our Dear Martin:

Don't forget grandma's birthday. She will be 64 on the 8th. American contributors will furnish 1,000 brushes for your German Young Painters' League. Mandelberg has joined in supporting the league. You must send 11 Picasso reproductions, 20 by 90 to branch galleries on the 25th, no sooner. Reds and blues must predominate. We can allow you $8,000 on this transaction at present. Start new accounts book 2.

Our prayers follow you daily, dear brother,

Eisenstein

EISENSTEIN GALLERIES
SAN FRANCISCO, CALIFORNIA, U.S.A.

January 17, 1934

Herrn Martin Schulse
Schloss Rantzenburg
Munich, Germany

Martin, Dear Brother:

Good news! Our stock reached 116 five days ago. The Fleishmans have advanced another $10,000. This will fill your Young Painters' League quota for a month but let us know if opportunities increase. Swiss miniatures are having a vogue. You must watch the market and plan to be in Zurich after May first if any unexpected opportunities develop. Uncle Solomon will be glad to see you and I know you will rely heavily on his judgment.

The weather is clear and there is little danger of storms during the next two months. You will prepare for your students the following reproductions: Van Gogh 15 by 103, red; Poussin 20 by 90, blue and yellow; Vermeer 11 by 33, red and blue.

Our hopes will follow your new efforts.

Eisenstein

EISENSTEIN GALLERIES
SAN FRANCISCO, CALIFORNIA, U.S.A.

January 29, 1934

Herrn Martin Schulse
Schloss Rantzenburg
Munich, Germany

Dear Martin:

Your last letter was delivered by mistake at 457 Geary St., Room 4. Aunt Rheba says tell Martin he must write more briefly and clearly so his friends can understand all that he says. I am sure everyone will be in readiness for your family reunion on the 15th. You will be tired after these festivities and may want to take your family with you on your trip to Zurich.

Before leaving however, procure the following reproductions for branches of German Young Painters' League, looking forward to the joint exhibit in May or earlier: Picasso 17 by 81, red; Van Gogh 5 by 42, white; Rubens 15 by 204, blue and yellow.

Our prayers are with you.

Eisenstein

SCHLOSSRANTZENBURG
MUNICH, GERMANY

February 12, 1934

Mr. Max Eisenstein
Eisenstein Galleries
San Francisco, California, U.S.A.

Max, My Old Friend:

My God, Max, do you know what you do? I shall have to try to smuggle this letter out with an American I have met here. I write an appeal from a despair you cannot imagine. This crazy cable! These letters you have sent. I am called in to account for them. The letters are not delivered, but they bring me in and show me letters from you and demand I give them the code. A code? And how can you, a friend of long years, do this to me?

Do you realize, have you any idea that you destroy me? Already the results of your madness are terrible. I am bluntly told I must resign my office. Heinrich is no longer in the boys' corps. They tell him it will not be good for his health. God in heaven, Max, do you see what that means? And Elsa, to whom I dare not tell anything, comes in bewildered that the officials refuse her invitations and Baron Von Freische does not speak to her upon the street.

Yes, yes, I know why you do it -- but do you not understand I could do nothing? What could I have done? I did not dare to try. I beg of you, not for myself, but for Elsa and the boys -- think what it means to them if I am taken away and they do not know if I live or die. Do you know what it is to be taken to a concentration camp? Would you stand me against a wall and level the gun? I beg of you, stop. Stop now, while everything is not yet destroyed. I am in fear for my life, for my life, Max.

Is it you who does this? It cannot be you. I have loved you like a brother, my old Maxel. My God, have you no mercy? I beg you, Max, no more, no more! Stop while I can be saved. From a heart filled with old affection I ask it.

Martin

EISENSTEIN GALLERIES
SAN FRANCISCO, CALIFORNIA, U.S.A.

February 15, 1934

Herrn Martin Schulse
Schloss Rantzenburg
Munich, Germany

Our Dear Martin:

Seven inches of rainfall here in 18 days. What a season! A shipment of 1,500 brushes should reach the Berlin branch for your painters by this weekend. This will allow time for practice before the big exhibition. American patrons will help with all the artists' supplies that can be provided, but you must make the final arrangements. We are too far out of touch with the European market and you are in a position to gauge the extent of support such a showing would arouse in Germany. Prepare these for distribution by March 24th: Rubens 12 by 77, blue; Giotto 1 by 317, green and white; Poussin 20 by 90, red and white.

Young Blum left last Friday with the Picasso specifications. He will leave oils in Hamburg and Leipzig and will then place himself at your disposal.

Success to you!
Eisenstein

EISENSTEIN GALLERIES
SAN FRANCISCO, CALIFORNIA, U.S.A.

March 3, 1934

Martin Our Brother:

Cousin Julius has two nine-pound boys. The family is happy. We regard the success of your coming artists' exhibition as assured. The last shipment of canvases was delayed due to difficulties of international exchange but will reach your Berlin associates in plenty of time. Consider reproduction collection complete. Your best support should come from Picasso enthusiasts but neglect no other lines.

We leave all final plans to your discretion but urge an early date for wholly successful exhibit.

The God of Moses be at your right hand.

Eisenstein

ABOUT THE AUTHOR

KRESSMANN TAYLOR (1903-1996) WON NATIONAL acclaim in 1939 with the publication of *Address Unknown.* She went on to write three more books and a dozen short stories, one of which was dramatized on *CBS Studio One*, and another was included in *The Best American Short Stories of 1956.* For nineteen years, she was a popular professor of creative writing and journalism at Gettysburg College in Pennsylvania, where she was the first woman to earn tenure.

APPENDIX A: BIOGRAPHY

———

Kressmann Taylor (1903 - 1996)

KATHRINE "KRESSMANN TAYLOR" ROOD, "THE woman who jolted America," was born Kathrine Kressmann in Portland, Oregon in 1903. Her father, Charles August Kressmann, was a banker, and a first-generation American, born in Chicago in 1870, only days after his Alsatian/ German parents arrived in the United States. Her mother, Susan Starr Kressmann, was a tenth-generation descendant of a New England family dating back to 1634 in Massachusetts and including Revolutionary War soldiers, early manufacturers, and a doctor who was one of the founders of Harvard University.

A precocious child, Kathrine won her first writing award at age eleven, First Prize in a contest for children up to age sixteen; with the prize money she bought herself a complete set of the *Book of Knowledge*. Graduating from high school at age seventeen, and the University of Oregon at 21 (with a double major in English literature and journalism), she then moved to San Francisco, where she worked as an advertising copy writer, in her spare time writing fiction and poetry for some small literary journals. In 1928 the editors of the *San Francisco Review*, a magazine she particularly liked, invited her to a party where she met Elliott Taylor, the dapper, successful, and engaging owner of his own advertising agency; they were married within two weeks. Three years later, when the Great Depression had put an end to both their jobs and the advertising industry, the couple bought a small farm in southern Oregon, where they literally "lived off the land," growing their own food and panning gold, taking their two small children, and adding a third (of four) in 1935.

In 1938 they moved to New York, where Elliott worked as a trade-paper editor, and Kathrine finished writing "Address Unknown," which was rejected by several major book and magazine publishers, including *Harper's, Atlantic Monthly* and *Esquire*, before Elliott showed it to *STORY* magazine editor Whit Burnett, who immediately wished to publish it. He and Elliott decided that the story was "too strong to appear under the name of a woman" and assigned Kathrine the literary pseudonym "Kressmann Taylor," a professional name she accepted and kept for the rest of her life, largely because of the success of *Address Unknown*.

When "Address Unknown" was first published in the United States, in *STORY* in September, 1938, it caused an immediate sensation. Within ten days of publication, the entire printing of that issue of *STORY* was sold out, and enthusiastic readers were mimeographing copies of the story to send to friends. National radio commentator Walter Winchell heartily recommended the story, and *Reader's Digest* magazine put aside its long-standing no-fiction rule to reprint the story for its more than three million readers.

In 1939, Simon & Schuster printed *Address Unknown* as a book and sold fifty thousand copies – a huge number in those years. *The New York Times Book Review* raved, "This modern story is perfection itself. It is the most effective indictment of Nazism to appear in fiction." The United States was at this time officially neutral, but many in America, including the Roosevelt administration, openly supported the British in their singular war against Hitler. So, when a young German cleric, who had fled religious persecution in the Fatherland to seek asylum in the New World, wished to tell his story and expose the clandestine Nazi domination of the Lutheran Church in Germany, the FBI was immediately engaged to arrange his secret meeting(s) with the most eminent anti-Nazi story-teller in the U.S., Kressmann Taylor, who took his real life story and fictionalized it into her next book, *Until That Day, 1942* (republished in 2003 as *Day of No Return* and in several foreign translations). All references to the original family were obscured or deleted to protect the young minister's parents and siblings, who were still in Germany under Nazi domination, and Kressmann Taylor did not even mention his real name to anyone for over fifty years.

With unofficial government backing and major private financial support, *Until That Day* would probably have had an early success to challenge that of *Address Unknown*, but before the book was off the press, the Japanese bombed Pearl Harbor, fascist-support sentiment dissolved in America, and the nation went to war. The book was well received and sold well, but did not have a second printing or paperback edition, and for the next sixty years was neither translated nor distributed beyond the U.S.

In 1942, Elliott and Kathrine moved to another farm, in Pennsylvania, near Gettysburg, where, because of her literary reputation, Kathrine was soon offered a guest lectureship in creative writing at Gettysburg College, a small Lutheran-related liberal arts college. Her first course attracted such student interest that she was offered a full-time instructorship after the first year, and she continued to teach there for nineteen years, becoming the first woman ever granted professorial status, and the first ever granted tenure.

Following the war, both *Address Unknown* and *Until That Day* slipped from public notice and were largely forgotten. Elliott Taylor died in 1953, and Kathrine lived on as a widow for the next thirteen years, continuing to write in the summers and to teach writing, journalism, and literary foundations at the college. During this period she published ten short stories and saw one of them dramatized on television, another selected for *Best American Short Stories of 1954*.

In 1966, Kathrine retired, sold the farm, and moved to Florence, Italy, where she experienced the great flood of the Arno river in

November of that year – resulting in her third book, *Diary of Florence in Flood*, published to critical acclaim in America and England (as *Ordeal By Water*) the following spring.

En route to this Italian "retirement" in 1966 on the Italian Lines' *Michelangelo*, Kathrine met the American sculptor John Rood. The two felt an immediate attraction, had a shipboard romance, and were married the following year in Minneapolis, Minnesota, where he made his home. Thereafter, they lived part of each year in Minneapolis, part in the Val de Pesa, outside Florence. Even after Rood's death in 1974, Kathrine kept both homes for many years, living quietly in each six months a year, simply as Mrs. John Rood.

Then, in 1995, when she was 91 years old, Story Press reissued *Address Unknown*, "to commemorate the 50th anniversary of the liberation of the concentration camps," and because, as *STORY* editor Lois Rosenthal wrote, its "significant and timeless message... has earned it a permanent place on the bookshelves" of America. The book was well received, and Kathrine, happily signing copies and granting television and press interviews, was gratified at its re-emergence, this time with the stature of a classic of American literature.

Kathrine Kressmann Taylor Rood died the following year, in July, 1996, late in her 93rd year, sharp-witted, perceptive, and enthusiastic about life until the end. Shortly after her death, a copy of *Address Unknown* came into the hands of the French publisher of Editions Autrement, Paris. He saw at once its relevance to the entire European community, both those who had lived under the Nazi domination and those who had not. He determined that a French translation must be undertaken, and that translation hit the French best-seller list in late 1999. Since then more than 600,000 copies have sold in France, and as of 2016, translations have been done in twenty-one other languages, around the world.

Demand from readers the world over for other works by Kathrine Kressmann Taylor led to republication of her second book, published in French in 2002 as *Jour sans retour*. Its popular reception in that edition led to extensive research and new background materials for a new updated edition, printed in German (*Bis zu jenem Tag*, 2002), in Italian (*Senza Ritorno*, 2003), and in English as *Day of No Return, 2004.*

One last book remained unpublished, her *Storm on the Rock*, written in 1978. She left the completed manuscript with her son Douglas before she died, telling him to see it published "if and when the time seems appropriate." As of 2016, it has been published only in French translation, as *Jours d'orage*, by Flammarion in 2008.

APPENDIX B

———

Kressmann Taylor Chronology:

August 19, 1903, born Kathrine Kressmann, Portland, Oregon

May, 1924, BA in English & Journalism, University of Oregon

June 2, 1928, married Elliott Taylor, San Francisco, California

May 27, 1930, daughter Helen Kressmann Taylor born, Redwood City, California

July 9, 1931, son Thomas Elliott Taylor born, Ross, California

March 4, 1935, son Charles Douglas Taylor born, Grant's Pass, Oregon

April, 1935, short story "Take a Carriage, Madam," published in, *Controversy*, under pseudonym Sarah B. Kennedy

September 1938, "Address Unknown" published in *STORY* magazine

July 13, 1939, son Jonathan Golding Taylor born, Tappan, New York

1939, *ADDRESS UNKNOWN*, book, published in US by Simon & Schuster, in UK by Hamish Hamilton

1942, *UNTIL THAT DAY* published by Eagle Books

1944, *ADDRESS UNKNOWN* film, Columbia Pictures

Sept. 1947, Guest lecturer, Gettysburg College, Gettysburg, Pennsylvania

1948 – 1966, Assoc. Prof., Gettysburg College, Gettysburg, Pennsylvania

Dec. 25, 1953, Elliott Taylor died, Gettysburg, Pennsylvania

1953 – 1965, during summer vacations, wrote 10 more short stories (included in *ELEVEN STORIES, Plus*)

August, 1966, retired from teaching, moved to Florence, Italy

1967, *DIARY OF FLORENCE IN FLOOD* published in US by Simon & Schuster, in UK by Hamish Hamilton as *ORDEAL BY WATER*

1967, married John Rood, Minneapolis, Minnesota, and settled near San Casciano, Val de Pesa, Tuscany

June 29, 1974, John Rood died, Minneapolis, Minnesota

1978, completed novel, *STORM ON THE ROCK,* (published in France as *JOURS D'ORAGE* in 2008)

1995, *ADDRESS UNKNOWN* commemorative edition published by STORY Press.

June 2, 1995, interview, *Northern Lights & Insights,* #342, Hennepin County Library,   Minnesota Public Television

1995, approved plan for first translation of *ADDRESS UNKNOWN* (into Hebrew) by Asher Tarmon, Israel

1996, Died July 14, Minneapolis, Minnesota

Books by Douglas and Catherine Taylor

HOW TO PILOT AN AEROPLANE, (1973, 1974, 1978; revised edition 1986) *General Aviation Press,* humor, by C. Douglas Taylor, dedicated to "Catherine Wright Taylor, one o the original Wright sisters."

FOOTBALL IN AMERICA, (2003), *Xlibris,* humorous novel by C. Douglas Taylor, cover art by Catherine Wright Taylor

DOWNTOWN DUCKS, (2003), *Xlibris,* by Douglas & Catherine Taylor; children's story by Douglas; watercolor illustrations by Catherine.

THE REACTOR, (2008), *Create Space,* novel by C. Douglas Taylor, cover art by Catherine Taylor

THANKSGIVING, (2012), *Create Space,* by Douglas & Catherine Taylor, children's book; poem by Douglas Taylor, watercolor illustrations by Catherine Taylor.

POETRY AND ART, (2015) *Create Space,* by Catherine & Douglas Taylor, poems by Douglas and reproductions of art and sculpture by Catherine Wright Taylor.

Made in the USA
Coppell, TX
13 December 2020